Don't Be Scared, Eleven

Story by Richard Thompson
Illustrated by Eugenie Fernandes

Annick Press
Toronto

"Helmet on?"
"Yes, Dad."
"Seat belt on?"
"Yes, Dad."
"All ready then?"

Jesse checked. She had two books and a bag of snacks. She had her pet elephant, Eleven. And she had her rock.

"Ready to go, Dad."

"What's this, Jesse?" asked her dad.

"That's my rock," said Jesse. "I'm making a collection."

"That's a big rock . . ." said her dad.

"I'm making a big collection," said Jesse.

"That rock is too heavy," said her dad. "I'm sorry. We'll have to leave it behind. I will get too tired pulling the trailer with a heavy rock in it."

"It's my favourite . . ." said Jesse sadly.

"I will help you look for a new rock when we get home," said her dad. "Okay?"

"Okay, Dad."

So the rock stayed, and they went—Jesse's mom and dad riding on their bikes, and Jesse and Eleven riding in their trailer.

On they rode.

"Jesse," said Eleven, "are we almost home?"

"Soon," said Jesse. "We have two more sleeps in our tent, and then we will be home."

"I miss home," said Eleven.

"I know," said Jesse. "Would you like me to read you a story?"

So Jesse read a story to her friend, and on they rode.

"Jesse," said Eleven, "is this a forest?"
There were a lot of trees around.
"Yes, Eleven."
"Are there bears?" asked Eleven, peeking
nervously over the top of the trailer.
"Don't worry," said Jesse. "I will sing you a song."
So Jesse put her arm around her elephant and
sang softly to him, and on they rode.

"Jesse," said Eleven, "we're going over a high bridge. Maybe we will fall in the water!"

"Don't be scared, Eleven," said Jesse. "Here. Let's have a snack. We'll eat some raisins and some carrots now, and we will save the apple and the gum drops for later."

So Jesse and her elephant shared a snack, and on they rode.

"Jesse," said Eleven, "Are we going up a mountain? Mountains are high. We might fall off!"

"Try to think happy thoughts, Eleven," said Jesse. "Let's snuggle down and have a nap."

So Jesse hugged Eleven, closed her eyes and went to sleep. But Eleven couldn't sleep.

He looked out and saw the road winding away far below. He saw the river at the bottom of the canyon.

"Don't be scared, Eleven," he said to himself. "Have a snack."

He ate the apple.

They were getting VERY high up. They were almost to the clouds.

"Don't be scared, Eleven," the little elephant told himself. "Have a snack."

He ate *all* the gum drops.

"Puff! Puff! Puff!"

Jesse's dad was getting out of breath.

"Boy, this trailer is getting heavy," he gasped. "I don't know if I can make it all the way up this mountain. Whew!"

He looked over his shoulder and . . .

"What!"

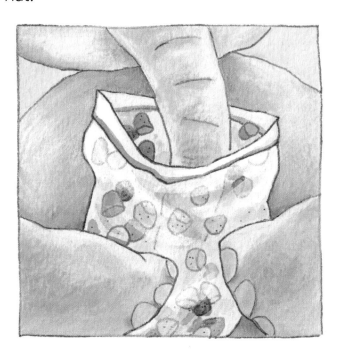

There was a two thousand kilogram elephant riding in the trailer with his daughter.

"He got so fat from eating ALL the gum drops, Dad," said Jesse.

"I was scared," said Eleven.

"Well, he's too heavy," said Jesse's dad. "I can't pull the trailer with that elephant riding. He'll have to walk behind."

"No!" cried Eleven. "You'll go too fast. I'll get lost. Please let me ride." Jesse's Dad shook his head.

"I have an idea," said Jesse.

That night when Jesse and her mom and dad were all asleep in the tent, Eleven heard a noise in the dark—a crick and a crack and a scrabble.

"Don't be scared, Eleven," the elephant whispered to himself. "Have a snack."

He snuffled his trunk into the food bag, and found . . .

. . . A WHOLE BAG OF MARSHMALLOWS!

© 1993 Richard Thompson (Text)
© 1993 Eugenie Fernandes (Art)
Annick Press Ltd.

Annick Press gratefully acknowledges the support
of The Canada Council and the Ontario Arts
Council.

Canadian Cataloguing in Publication Data

Thompson, Richard, 1951–
   Don't be scared, Eleven

(The Jesse adventure series)
ISBN 1-55037-286-6 (bound)
ISBN 1-55037-287-4 (pbk.)

I. Fernandes, Eugenie, 1943–   . II. Title.
III. Series: Thompson, Richard, 1951–   .
The Jesse adventures.

PS8589.H65D66 1993   jC813'.54   C92-094637-2
PZ7.T46Do   1993

The art in this book was rendered in gouache,
water colour pencil and ink. The type was set in
Kabel book by Attic Typesetting.

Distribution for Canada and The USA:
Firefly Books Ltd.,
250 Sparks Avenue
North York, Ontario   M2H 2S4

∞ Printed on Acid-Free Paper

Printed and bound in Canada
by D.W. Friesen & Sons, Altona, Manitoba